A Chartreuse Leotard in a Magenta Limousine

And Other Words Named After People and Places

Lynda Graham-Barber

Illustrated by Barbara Lehman

Hyperion Books for Children
New York

For Mom, who looks great in chartreuse
—L.G.B.

To Dave Passalaqua
—B.L.

Text © 1994 by Lynda Graham-Barber. Illustrations © 1994 by Barbara Lehman.
All rights reserved. Printed in the United States of America.
For information address Hyperion Books for Children,
114 Fifth Avenue, New York, New York 10011.

FIRST EDITION

1 3 5 7 9 10 8 6 4 2

Library of Congress Cataloging-in-Publication Data

Graham-Barber, Lynda.
A chartreuse leotard in a magenta limousine/Lynda Graham-Barber;
illustrated by Barbara Lehman.
p. cm.
ISBN 0-7868-0003-8 (trade) 0-7868-2002-0 (lib. bdg.)
1. English language—Etymology—Juvenile literature.   2. English
language—Eponyms—Juvenile literature.   3. Names, Geographical—
Juvenile literature.   I. Lehman, Barbara.   II. Title.
PE1574.G73   1994
422—dc20   94-8597 CIP AC

contents

introduction

Many of our English words developed from Greek and Latin sources. One such word is *eponym*. *Eponym* comes from two Greek words, *epi*, "after," and *onyma*, "name." A word that develops "after a name" is called an eponym. *Eponym*, then, is just a fancy term for a word "named after" a person.

Chances are you use eponyms all the time without even realizing it. Did you know, for example, the Teddy behind the huggable stuffed teddy bear was President Theodore "Teddy" Roosevelt? French trapeze artist Jules Léotard gave his name to the clinging leotard he invented, while the whizzing Frisbee borrowed its trademark from a New England baker named William Frisbie.

A close cousin of the eponym is the toponym. *Toponym* also has Greek roots, coming from *topos*, "place," and *onyma*, "name." A word that develops from a "place name" is called a toponym. Like eponyms, many toponyms are part of our everyday language.

It's easy to figure out some toponym hometowns. The hamburger's name came directly from Hamburg, Germany, where the first hamburger sizzled. Butchers in Bologna, Italy, stuffed what became known as bologna sausage. Some toponyms, however, are not as obvious—mayonnaise took its name from Mahón, Spain, and denim is named after Nîmes, France.

The stories behind eponyms and toponyms make for fascinating reading. Chances are good that today you'll either wear, eat, or use something that got its name from the person or place that inspired it. And contrary to what you might think, people who have things named after them are not always inventors or scientists. They're musicians, acrobats, tailors, rent collectors, and even school-age children. Likewise, the sources for place names are surprisingly varied, from exotic islands and lavish estates to typical small towns and simple monasteries.

So put on your magenta polka-dot jersey (that's three different stories), grab a bologna sandwich (there's two more), and get ready to explore the world of eponyms and toponyms.

ferris wheels and frisbees

olympic

toponym: Olympia, Greece

Did you realize the original Olympic Games were held nearly three thousand years ago, millennia before television networks competed for satellite broadcasting rights? The games are called the Olympics because the Greeks held athletic contests at Olympia, a religious center in southern Greece.

At those first games, in 776 B.C., the 200-yard sprint was the lone event, and only men were allowed to compete. Over a thousand years later, the contest was suspended because it was considered pagan. In 1896 the Greek games were resurrected, thanks to the efforts of French baron Pierre de Coubertin.

The 1992 Summer Olympic Games at Barcelona featured 28 sports, with 250 individual medal events. Women first competed in the Olympic Games in 1900.

marathon

toponym: Marathon, Greece

When most of us think of marathons, sweat, sneakers, and sore muscles come to mind. Yet any event that extends over a long time is called a marathon, whether a congressional speech or a fund-raising car wash.

The word *marathon* comes from Marathon, an ancient town in northeastern Greece. In 490 B.C. the Greek army defeated the invading Persians at Marathon. After the Greeks won, a young Athenian named Pheidippides ran 20 miles from Marathon to Athens to spread the good news, only to die from exhaustion.

Many believe it was to honor Pheidippides' effort that officials sponsored a 20-mile race from Marathon to Athens in the 1896 Olympic Games. The present marathon distance of 26 miles, 385 yards (42.2 kilometers) was set at the 1908 Olympic Games in London. Women first ran in an Olympic marathon in 1984.

nike

eponym: Nike, Greek goddess

At their athletic and military contests the Greeks always displayed a statue of Nike, the goddess of victory, to inspire the competitors. Therefore it's not surprising that after the impressive Greek victory at Marathon, Nike's popularity hit an all-time high.

In 1962, nearly 2,500 years after Nike brought good fortune to the Greeks at Marathon, a University of Oregon runner and his coach came up with an improved design for athletic sneakers. They named their waffle-soled, cushioned shoe Nike, after the Greek goddess of victory.

In the 1972 Olympic trials marathon runners wearing the new custom-made Nikes placed among the top ten finishers. Today one out of three pairs of running shoes sold are Nikes.

rugby

toponym: Rugby School, England

Soccer fans know that the one thing you must never do is touch the ball with your hands or arms during play. But, as the story goes, that's exactly what one frustrated young man did at Rugby School in England in 1823: during a soccer match, he caught the ball and tore down the field. The sport of running with the ball caught on as an alternative to soccer and became known as rugby, after the school where it was first played.

The Super Bowl owes a big debt to rugby, for American football developed from its English cousin in the mid-1800s. Both are considered rough sports, but there are several differences between football and rugby. Rugby players do not wear protective gear, and they are not allowed to block, throw forward passes, take time-outs, or make substitutions.

badminton
toponym: Badminton House, England

Quick, after soccer, what's the second most popular world-participation sport? Hint: it's a game played with rackets and a net. No, not tennis. Surprise!—it's badminton (minton, not mitten), that lazy-summer-day backyard pastime. It also might surprise you that badminton shuttlecocks (also called birdies) have been clocked going over the net at a not-so-lazy 200 miles an hour in world-class competitions.

By best estimates, badminton was first played in India by British army officers in the 1860s. The game was called *poona,* named after Poona, a city south of Bombay. In the following decade returning officers took the sport back with them to England. About a hundred miles northwest of London, in Gloucester, the first birdies whizzed at the duke of Beaufort's estate. The game became known as badminton after the duke's house, Badminton.

An instant hit in England, badminton quickly traveled to the United States in the 1870s. Badminton became an official Olympic Games medal sport for the first time during the 1992 Summer Olympic Games in Barcelona.

frisbee

eponym: William Frisbie

An expert Frisbee player can toss a flying disk an unbelievable 230 feet. There is even a movement to make flying disk a future Olympic event. But did you know that the first Frisbee was an empty metal pie tin from a Bridgeport, Connecticut, bakery, which baked its first pie more than a hundred years ago?

We'll never know whose idea it was to spin an empty tin with the name of William Frisbie's bakery embossed on the bottom. But by the 1940s tossing Frisbie pie tins was a favorite pastime at nearby Yale University. The college kids called the sport Frisbie-ing.

Frisbie flying took off commercially in 1948 when Walter Morrison, a young UFO enthusiast from California, shaped a plastic disk to resemble a flying saucer. In 1957 the Wham-O Toy Company marketed the disks as toy flying saucers under the name Frisbee.

raggedy ann

eponym: **Ragamuffin**

Small-scale representations of human forms weren't always considered playthings for young children. Three thousand years ago in Egypt, grieving Egyptians put clay figures in their loved ones' tombs to keep them company. Some thousand years later, children began dressing and cradling toy babies with movable joints. Over the centuries that followed, these figures were fashioned out of corn husks, wood, china, and even scraps of rag.

One of the most beloved rag toys is Raggedy Ann, with her long mop of bright red hair and patchwork clothing. It's thought that Raggedy Ann inherited her name from Ragamoffyn, a character that appeared in a late-fourteenth-century poem called *Piers Plowman.* Now we use the term *ragamuffin* to describe someone who dresses shabbily, like Raggedy Ann.

By 1700 toys like Raggedy Ann were called dolls. The story behind the word *doll* is a curious one and certainly relates to our discussion of words named after people and places. Word historians agree that *doll* is actually an abbreviation, or pet name, for the name Dorothy (Dor became Dol, then Doll.) Why the toys were called "Dolls" rather than, say, "Katies" or "Beths," no one knows.

barbie and ken dolls

The identity of the Dorothy behind *doll* is a mystery, but there's no question about the real people behind the Barbie- and Ken-doll names. In 1958 the owners of the Mattel Toy Company, the Handlers, designed a doll with a trendy wardrobe for their young daughter Barbie, who preferred playing with grown-up-looking dolls. Three years after Barbie's sensational debut, Mattel introduced Barbie's boyfriend, Ken. Following the precedent set by Barbie, the doll was named after the Handlers' son, Ken.

teddy bear   eponym: President Theodore Roosevelt

Yes, there is a very famous Teddy and a real black bear behind the stuffed teddy bear's name—and a bittersweet story.

When President Theodore Roosevelt went bear hunting in Mississippi in 1902, he refused to shoot a Louisiana black bear cornered by 20 hound dogs. Taking pity on the old, lame animal, Roosevelt instructed a companion to kill the bear to end its suffering. When the story broke, an enterprising Brooklyn candy store owner named Morris Michtom put in his window a small stuffed bear labeled "Teddy's bear."

Everyone wanted a huggable bear, so Michtom got the president's permission to borrow his nickname: "Teddy." By the time Michtom died in 1938, his Ideal Novelty and Toy Company was stuffing more than 100,000 teddy bears a year.

ferris wheel   eponym: George Ferris

Next to the roller coaster, the star attraction at many amusement parks is the stomach-churning, upside-down-spinning Ferris wheel. The large power-driven, revolving wheels are usually about 50 feet in diameter and can be assembled and dismantled in only a few hours.

The popular amusement ride got its name from American inventor and engineer George Washington Gale Ferris, who designed the first Ferris wheel. The giant observation wheel made its maiden revolution on June 21, 1893, at the World's Columbian Exposition in Chicago. It was 250 feet in diameter and had a capacity of 2,160 squealing passengers. The highest Ferris wheel in operation today is in Yokohama, Japan. It is 328 feet in diameter and can accommodate 480 people.

catherine wheel

eponym: Saint Catherine

You don't have to take a ride on a mechanized Ferris wheel to flip upside down. Under your own power, you can do a sideways somersault, also called a cartwheel. Another not-so-common name for this cartwheel is a Catherine wheel. A Catherine wheel is used to describe a type of firework that gives off colorful sparks as it spins, as well as a popular toy, also called a pinwheel.

The Catherine who gave her name to both these entertainments lived in Alexandria, Egypt, in the fourth century. After refusing to publicly disclaim her Christian beliefs, young Catherine was tortured on a hideous device with a rotating spiked wheel, before being beheaded. Declared a saint, Catherine was adopted as the patron saint of wheelwrights, those people who make and repair vehicle wheels.

nelson

toponym: Nelson, England

The first recorded wrestling match took place in Japan, in 23 B.C. Evidence indicates that wrestling was also a major sport in ancient Egypt and Greece. Although there are several different styles of wrestling, the final goal is the same: to pin both shoulders of your opponent to the floor.

In one wrestling hold called a nelson, wrestlers pass one or both arms under the opponents' arms from behind and then apply pressure on the neck. There are full nelsons, double nelsons, half nelsons, and even three-quarter nelsons.

We can't be sure how the hold got its name, but most likely it came from the Lancashire town Nelson, which, in turn, got its name from the eighteenth-century English admiral Viscount Horatio Nelson.

charleston

toponym: Charleston, South Carolina

Set to lively leg-kicking rhythms, the Charleston was one of the most popular ballroom dances of the 1920s flapper era. The dance got its name from the place where it originated, Charleston, South Carolina. The city of Charleston was, like Nelson, England, named after a celebrated person. In 1670 the English founders called the city Charleston after their king, Charles II.

The energetic, rigorous music composed in 4/4 time for the Charleston had a great influence on the 1940s jitterbug and ten years later, on rock-and-roll music.

dodgers   eponym: The Artful Dodger

In English novelist Charles Dickens's *Oliver Twist,* Jack Dawkins darted in and out of crowds picking pockets, always one step ahead of the London police. For this skill he was nicknamed the Artful Dodger. Generally speaking, you dodge something when you move quickly to avoid it. It could be a volleyball, an avalanche, or the military draft.

But the famous Brooklyn Dodgers didn't get their name because they dodged baseballs. Their home stadium, Ebbets Field, was built in the 1880s near a maze of trolley tracks. To get to the ballpark, fans dodged the trolley cars, just as Jack Dawkins dodged through London. The Brooklyn team became known as the Brooklyn Dodgers after their trolley-dodging fans.

saxophone

The saxophone took its name from Antoine J. Sax, who was known as Adolphe. Sax was a Belgian musical instrument maker who built the first saxophone, the only reed woodwind instrument made entirely of metal. The eponymous saxophone has generally been overlooked by most serious composers but is considered a mainstay of both jazz and popular music. Over seventy years ago, orchestras that played the Charleston included up to five different saxophonists, on alto, tenor, and baritone horn.

music

eponym: Greek Muses

Did you ever hear someone hoping for inspiration say, "I'm waiting for the Muse to strike"? The phrase refers to the Muses, the name for the nine daughters of Zeus, the supreme Greek god. The nine sisters each represented a different art or science: music, tragedy, comedy, choral song and dance, astronomy, poetry (epic, love, sacred), and history.

Our word *music* developed from the collective name for these nine daughters of Zeus and Mnemosyne (neh-má-sin-ee), the goddess of memory. The word *mnemonic* comes from Mnemosyne. It refers to any device that helps one to remember something. One example is the phrase *Every Good Boy Does Fine*, with EGBDF referring to the notes on the treble staff in music.

Since the Muses cover so many different art forms, you can call on them whether you're contemplating a silly sonnet, a science fiction novel, or a planet. And once you get a good idea, don't forget to ask Mnemosyne to help you remember it!

vaudeville

toponym: Vau de Vire, France

While the Charleston and saxophones were setting toes tapping, vaudeville acts were traveling across America and Europe, performing a blend of pantomime, dance, song, acrobatics, comedy, and trained-animal acts.

The word *vaudeville* has its roots in France. Years ago the people of Normandy wrote songs known as *chansons du vau-de-Vire*, or "songs of the valley of Vire." Later, the name changed to "valley of the town"; in French, *vau de ville.*

The first vaudeville shows in the United States appeared in Boston in 1885. In 1910 there were 31 vaudeville theaters in New York City alone. The largest ones featured up to 20 acts during a performance. By 1932 there were no vaudeville houses left. Most of them had been converted into movie theaters.

tarantella

Little Miss Muffet isn't alone. Many people are afraid of spiders. Hundreds of years ago a small town in southeastern Italy was so overrun with tarantula spiders that it was named Taranto after the spider infestation.

Local people in Taranto believed that those who received the painful but not deadly bite of the huge, hairy spiders would suffer delirium or melancholy. They thought the cure was to twirl around in a frenzied, rollicking dance, while

local musicians played guitar, castanets, or tambourine. This therapeutic folk dance, in 6/8 time, became known as the tarantella after the town named after a spider.

spa

Health spas today attract people who want to keep fit through exercise and diet. However, in centuries past, visitors to spas were usually sick people in search of a cure for a specific health problem.

The word *spa* comes from an actual town in Belgium called Spa. In Spa, clients took therapeutic baths and drank healing waters from the natural springs, which were rich in magnesium, calcium, iron, bicarbonate, fluoride, and iodine.

The use of mineral springs for therapy goes back to the fifth century B.C., when hot springs in Greece and the Aegean islands were healing centers. Spas built by the Romans still exist in Bath, England, and Baden, Germany. The name of Bath, the city famous for its therapeutic hot baths, and our word *bath* derive from the same Old English verb, *bacan*. The meaning of *bacan* was "to bake," which might describe the effect of the bath's water temperature on some of the bathers.

hooligans, vandals, and regular guys

zealot

eponym: Zealot sect

Someone might call you a zealot if you're passionately devoted to a cause or a pursuit. It could be collecting baseball cards, playing Frisbee, or saving the whales. The word was coined after a group of people called the Zealots, who lived in the first century A.D. in ancient Palestine.

For many years the Zealots fought the Romans to keep their Palestine homeland free from Roman occupation. However, in A.D. 73 the Zealots lost their battle when, despite zealous efforts, they failed to defend the rock fortress at Masada on the Dead Sea. Rather than surrender to the Roman army, 960 Zealots committed suicide.

siren

eponym: Greek Sirens

Did you ever hear a beautiful woman with lots of sex appeal referred to as a siren? Marilyn Monroe was certainly one. The word *siren* comes directly from the mythological creatures in Greek lore called the Sirens.

According to legend these part-female, part-bird creatures bewitched men with their sweet singing. It's believed that some listeners became so spellbound that they forgot to eat and hence died of hunger. In the Greek stories sailors often fell victim to the Sirens. Odysseus, the Greek hero of Homer's epic poem the *Odyssey,* plugged his sailors' ears with beeswax and tied himself to the mast when his ship passed the Sirens. Deaf to their mesmerizing songs, Odysseus's crew sailed safely by.

tantalize

eponym: Tantalus, Greek king

If you dangle catnip within reach of your cat, Whiskers, then yank it away when Whiskers jumps, you are teasing, or tantalizing, your cat. Like *siren, tantalize* is another word with its roots in Greek mythology.

The legendary Greek king Tantalus had a problem similar to Whiskers's. The chief god, Zeus, banished Tantalus to Hades for theft. Condemned to stand beneath well-laden fruit trees, up to his chin in a pool of water under a huge hanging rock, Tantalus got very hungry and thirsty. But whenever Tantalus tried to eat the fruit dangling over his head, it flew out of reach. If the king tried to drink, the water level dropped, and Zeus threatened to let the rock topple down and crush Tantalus.

berserk

eponym: bear-sark

When people lose control they are sometimes said to go berserk. Most eponyms take their names from one individual. *Berserk,* like *zealot,* is an exception. *Berserk* came into the English language after the name for a group of powerful, courageous Norse warriors who lived in Scandinavia more than a thousand years ago.

In Old Norse these fighters were called *bear-sarks,* or "bear coats," because they fought wearing the skins from bears they had slain. The spelling of *bear-sark* was later changed to *berserkr.* These bear-coated warriors had a reputation for attacking their enemies in such a wild frenzy that they were thought to be indestructible.

vandal

eponym: Vandals

The morning headlines read: "Suspects Nabbed Vandalizing Mailboxes on Red Fox Road." Another word for a person who destroys or damages property is *vandal.* The word *vandal* goes back to the very first Vandals, a group of people who lived nearly two thousand years ago.

With a reputation for brutality similar to the bear-sarks', the Vandals were a Germanic tribe from an area that is now southern Poland. On their march, the feared Vandals overran much of western Europe and northern Africa, conquering and looting cities as they moved. After the tribe sacked Rome in A.D. 455 the word *vandal* was forever linked with acts of deliberate destruction.

hooligan

eponym: Patrick Hooligan and others

Unlike the words *berserk* and *vandal*, *hooligan*'s history is up for grabs. There are several stories surrounding the word *hooligan,* a name for a rough character who causes trouble. None of the tales are confirmable, but all are colorful.

One possibility is that *hooligan* evolved from the name of an Irish trouble-maker, Patrick Hooligan, who lived in the Southwark area of London at the turn of the century. Details of Hooligan's escapades, however, are sketchy at best. Other word experts claim *hooligan* first turned up in newspaper accounts from 1898 that told of an unruly bunch called Hooley's gang. A third theory is that the word came from comic song lyrics from the 1890s about a silly Irishman whose last name was Hooligan.

guy

eponym: Guy Fawkes

Why, you might ask, is *guy* tucked in among words that deal with riot and destruction? The reason is simple: the story behind the man behind the word is wrapped in intrigue and violence.

Guy Fawkes, the Englishman who gave his name to the word *guy,* may have been the original bad guy! Fawkes was in charge of setting off explosives that had been planted in the basement of London's House of Lords on November 5, 1605. Fawkes was arrested before he had time to light the fuse and was later hanged for his offense. Had the gunpowder exploded, King James I, among many others, would probably have died.

The failure of what later became known as the Gunpowder Plot is still cele-brated in England today, by burning effigies of villainous Guy Fawkes on November 5. In the mid-1800s, when the term was first coined in the United States, a *guy* meant a fellow. And gone were all the negative associations with conspiracy and death. Today, *guys* in the plural usually includes both sexes.

pandemonium

Pandemonium, Hades

What happens when everyone at a stadium tries to leave at the same time? Mass confusion, right? Another word to describe this chaos is *pandemonium*. And like *tantalize*, the word *pandemonium* has origins that involve the mythological lower region of Hades.

Seventeenth-century English religious scholar and poet John Milton's long poem *Paradise Lost* tells of Adam and Eve and their struggle with Satan. In the poem, Pandemonium (Greek for all the demons) is the capital city of Hades. Considered the center of wickedness, confusion reigned in the city of Pandemonium. By the 1860s *pandemonium* had evolved to mean any wild uproar.

16

clink
toponym: Clink Prison, London, England

Around Halloween did you ever drag metal chains over a hard surface to scare someone? If you did, what kind of sound did the chains make? A clanging—or maybe clinking—noise?

In the middle of the sixteenth century in Europe, jailed prisoners were typically chained in stone cells. It's thought the clinking sound made by their dragging chains was the inspiration behind calling one particular London prison in Southwark (Patrick Hooligan's stomping grounds!) Clink Prison. Later, *clink* became a slang term for any jail or prison. In old cowboy movies two popular slang words for prison are *pokey* and *hoosegow.* Word sleuths have few clues about *pokey*'s origins, but *hoosegow* is the Americanized pronunciation of the Mexican-Spanish word for courtroom, *juzgao* (whoze-gow). Can you think of any other slang words for prison?

duffel
toponym: Duffel, Belgium

When some people travel, they stuff their gear into large nylon or cotton carryalls called duffel bags. The first duffel bags, made of wool, were invented by the United States military. Today every enlisted soldier is issued one of these green sausage-shaped carriers.

Duffel bags were named after a woolen fabric called duffel. A coarse wool, duffel was first woven in Duffel, a town in Belgium, which then gave its name to the fabric totes. Because of its thick nap, the fabric was also made into coats and blankets, which were both durable and warm. The military duffel bags manufactured today are usually made of canvas instead of wool.

jeep
eponym: Eugene the Jeep

The crossword puzzle clue is "a four-letter word for an army vehicle beginning with *j.*" Right—*jeep!* Since 1940 the jeep has been the official all-purpose vehicle of the United States Army. The most widely accepted theory behind the jeep's name is that the term to describe it—*general purpose*—was abbreviated to g.p. Repeat g.p. quickly and you end up with a word that sounds like *jeep.*

It's also very likely that the army adopted the name jeep from a popular cartoon creature called "Eugene the Jeep." Making his debut in a Popeye cartoon strip in 1936, Eugene was, like Popeye, all-powerful and resourceful. Yes, you're right, this eponym is kind of a cheat—but it's fun.

dumdum

toponym: Dum Dum, India

Dumdum is a toponym that came into our language from India. A dumdum is a bullet with a soft or hollow nose that expands on impact, causing an especially ugly wound. The first dumdum was manufactured in 1897 at an ammunition factory in Dum Dum, a district of West Bengal, India.

Fighters in India first fired the bullets during the Indian frontier wars. Although dumdum bullets were strictly outlawed by a declaration of the first Hague conference, in 1899, they were reportedly used by both sides in World War I.

shrapnel

eponym: Henry Shrapnel

Another very destructive weapon used in war is the shrapnel shell. It is filled with explosive powder and lead balls and bursts in flight. This deadly shell was invented in 1784 by a young British army officer named Henry Shrapnel. The British army first fired shrapnel 20 years later while fighting the Dutch in Dutch Guiana, now Suriname.

Some historians believe shrapnel played a deciding role in one of the most famous battles in history, the Battle of Waterloo, in 1815. At Waterloo, the allies, led by the English duke of Wellington, used shrapnel in defeating the French forces commanded by Napoléon Bonaparte.

quonset hut

toponym: Quonset Point Naval Air Station, Rhode Island

Originally built by the United States Navy in 1941, Quonset huts provided temporary shelter for people and goods. The biggest advantage to these half-cylindrical corrugated steel structures was that they could be quickly assembled and taken apart.

The prefabricated huts got their name from Quonset Point Naval Air Station, where they were first made. The station in turn was named after the town, Quonset Point, Rhode Island. Quonset is a shortened version of the Narraganset word *seconquonset,* which means "land that juts into the water."

zeppelin eponym: Count Ferdinand von Zeppelin

Did you ever see a large football-shaped balloon decorated with a company name or advertisement hovering in the sky? This balloon is called a blimp, a kind of dirigible.

Dirigibles get their lift from gases and can be steered independently of the wind. Another kind of dirigible, more rigid than a blimp, is called a zeppelin. Zeppelins were named after their inventor, German count Ferdinand von Zeppelin.

Count Zeppelin's first dirigible flew for only 20 minutes in 1914. The most famous dirigible was the *Hindenburg*, which caught fire and crashed in 1937, in Lakehurst, New Jersey, killing 36 passengers. The largest zeppelin, at 800 feet long, the *Hindenburg* made several transatlantic flights before crashing.

guillotine

If you've ever used a good idea how the sharp machines for beheading tury, but it is with eighteenth-century There, during the Reign of Terror, the sands of French people; eventually Antoinette, lost their heads in 1793.

The man who designed this device The machine was originally called doctor. How, then, did the louisette of Doctor Louis named Doctor Jo- to use the louisette to execute all tence, not just aristocrats. Shortly af- name—the guillotine.

eponym: Doctor Joseph Guillotin

paper cutter at school, you have a blade of a guillotine works. Grisly people existed in the fourteenth cen- France that they are most identified. guillotine was used to execute thou- even Louis XVI and his wife, Marie

was French physician Doctor Louis. the *louisette* after the inventor- become the guillotine? A colleague seph Guillotin pleaded with officials French citizens under death sen- terward, the louisette got a new

boycott

eponym: Charles Boycott

If you refuse to eat tuna fish to protest the tuna processors who catch dolphins in their nets, you are staging a boycott. The person behind the word *boycott* was a retired British army officer named Captain Charles Boycott. But contrary to what you might expect, Captain Boycott didn't organize the first boycott, he was the object of one.

It was Captain Boycott's job to set and collect taxes for a wealthy Irish land-owner. In 1880, the tenants on Lord Erne's estates got so angry over the high rents that they refused to work until Boycott lowered the rates. To put more pressure on him, his servants deserted him, and tenants blocked his food supply. Captain Boycott had little choice but to reduce the rents. The word *boycott* was coined almost immediately in England to describe acts of resistance.

stonewall

eponym: General Thomas "Stonewall" Jackson

The tenants on Lord Erne's estates refused to work until Captain Boycott gave in. This kind of stubborn resistance can also be called stonewalling.

The person behind this tactic was a general in the Confederate army during the American Civil War, Thomas Jonathan Jackson. General Jackson earned the nickname "Stonewall" at the first battle of Bull Run, Virginia, on July 21, 1861. While Confederate soldiers fell back before a strong Union attack along the Bull Run Brook, the general's brigade refused to yield. One amazed Yankee general observed that the men stood firm "like a stone wall."

slave

toponym: Slavonia

In 1992, Yugoslavia made headlines all over the world when ethnic fighting broke out among Bosnian Croats, Serbs, and Muslims. *Slavs* is a term that originally referred to the people from Slavonia, a region in what was formerly northern Yugoslavia, now in Croatia.

The word *slave* has an ironic, even tragic, evolution. Originally *slav* meant "glory" in the Slavic language. This changed sometime during the Middle Ages (A.D. 500–1500), when invading hordes of Germans and Venetians overran Slavonia and took thousands of Slav fighters prisoner. With so many proud Slavs in captivity, the meaning of the word reversed to describe a person forced to serve another.

martinet

People in the armed forces have to conform to many rules, without questioning authority. So it should come as no surprise that the marquis de Martinet, the person behind the word that means a strict disciplinarian, was a French army officer.

As commander of King Louis XIV's personal regiment, Martinet came up with his own distinctive way of training officers. He did this by enforcing long stretches of continuous and rigorous drilling. So successful were the marquis's methods that his surname was eventually adopted to describe anyone who made people walk a straight, sometimes narrow, line.

guppies, guinea pigs, and guernseys

guppy
eponym: Robert John Lechmere Guppy

If you've ever visited an aquarium or had a fish tank of your own, chances are you've seen guppies. Their brilliant coloring and high reproductive rate make these two-inch-long fish a favorite pet. Another name for guppies is rainbow fish.

A minister from the West Indian island of Trinidad was the first to bring guppies to the attention of the world when he shipped a few fish to the British Museum in the late 1800s. His name was Robert John Lechmere Guppy. Since Guppy was credited with first discovering the small fish, guppies were named after the minister.

Nearly all fish hatch their young from eggs, but guppies are a rare exception. They bear live young, the way most mammals do.

guinea pig
toponym: Guiana, South America

Maybe you've seen pet guinea pigs in your schoolroom or the pet shop. Word experts agree that no one knows for sure why these small, almost tailless, domesticated rodents are called pigs. One explanation is that someone thought they looked like the young of an established breed of pigs called Guinea hogs.

The German word for guinea pig, *Meerschweinchen,* translates as "little pig from over the sea." This is a clue to another theory, that the rodents were named by European sailors who carried back the wild animals from the Guiana coast in northern South America. In English, the spelling of *Guiana* was changed to Guinea. Nowadays *guinea pig* is a slang term for someone who, willingly or unwillingly, is used in experimental testing.

saint bernard

toponym: Grand Saint Bernard hospice, Switzerland

Despite its impressive 170-pound weight, the powerful Saint Bernard has a gentle, kindly disposition. The huge dog with the sad eyes got its name from a travelers' lodge in the Swiss Alps named Grand Saint Bernard.

At the Grand Saint Bernard hospice, the resident monks trained the large dogs to find and rescue travelers stranded in the deep drifts of the Alpine passes. Since rescue work began 300 years ago, Saint Bernards are credited with saving over 2,000 lives. Originally called the Alpine dog, the protective Saint Bernard is typically depicted with a small wooden barrel hanging around its neck. The barrel supposedly contained brandy to warm the chilled travelers.

alaskan malamute

eponym: Malamute people

Have you read or seen clips on television about an annual 1,050-mile Alaskan dogsled race between Anchorage and Nome called the Iditarod? Some of the dogs that pull the sleds during the grueling endurance trek are malamutes. These powerful dogs got their name from the people who first bred them, the Malamutes of northwestern Alaska.

Alaskan malamutes are sometimes confused with Siberian huskies. Both have a bushy curled tail and a thick fur coat, and they excel as hauling animals. The huskies, however, have more variety in their coat color and, in some cases, pale, milky blue eyes.

canary

toponym: Canary Islands, Spain

The bright yellow birds called canaries were named after their island home, which was, in turn, named after native dogs. Here's how it happened.

When explorers first arrived on the chain of seven islands in the Atlantic Ocean off northwestern Africa, they found the islands overrun with large wild dogs. Since the Latin word for dog is *canis,* the islands later became known as the Canary Islands (Latin *Canaria Insula,* "Isle of Dogs") after these canines.

Explorers were also attracted by a streaky olive-green bird with a sweet song. Shipped to Europe, the wild birds were bred for more brilliant yellow plumage and named canaries after the Spanish-owned Canary Islands.

afghan hound

The Afghan hound is one of the oldest breeds of dogs in existence, dating as far back as 3000 B.C. Although the Afghan took its name from the Asian country of Afghanistan, it's believed the breed originated in Sinai, which is now part of Jordan and Egypt. For centuries, game hunters in the Near East put the dogs to work in tracking leopard and gazelle.

When chasing down these fleet-footed animals, the Afghan used its long, thin legs and muscular hindquarters. The Afghan is now admired by dog lovers more for its multicolored long, soft, flowing coat than its hunting speed.

A knitted or crocheted blanket is also called an afghan (lowercase), after the same country as the Afghan. If an Afghan curls up on an afghan, two toponyms are cuddling together.

pekingese

toponym: Peking, China

Most historians regard the 1,000-year-old T'ang dynasty as the golden age of Chinese civilization. During this time, the Chinese emperors kept lion dogs in the Imperial Palace. These huge, shaggy dogs, which weighed nearly 200 pounds, were held sacred by their royal masters.

In the mid-1800s, an admirer took five lion dogs to England. They were called Pekingese after their Chinese homeland. After a few decades of breeding, the dogs still had their long coats but had shed about 180 pounds. The lion dogs ended up as the Pekingese we see today, 14-pound pets that would fit comfortably in a lion's lap.

angora
toponym: Angora, Turkey

Did you ever touch a muff or a hat that was so soft and fuzzy it felt just like a kitten? It was probably made of angora or mohair.

In 1923 Turkey's first president, Kemal Atatürk, moved the country's capital seat from Constantinople to Angora. Even before Atatürk made Angora (now Ankara) the capital, the area was already well known as the place where cats, rabbits, and goats with beautiful coats were bred. These animals were called Angoras after their homeland.

Prized by cat fanciers, Angora cats are noted for their soft, long coats and plumelike tails. Because Angora rabbit hair is so soft, it's a popular textile in making women's sweaters, hats, gloves, and coats.

clydesdale
toponym: Clydesdale, Lanarkshire, Scotland

You may have spotted a team of sturdily built horses pulling a wagon advertising a famous beverage on television commercials. Or maybe you saw the horses during one of their annual cross-country tours. These proud, spirited animals are members of a breed called Clydesdales.

Bred from Flemish stock, the Clydesdales were named after Scotland's south-central Clyde River valley, where the breed was introduced around 150 years ago. Clydesdales are usually bay and brown in color with heavy white markings on their faces and legs. Like Percheron and Belgian horses, Clydesdales are referred to as work, or draft, horses. During the last century, farmers harnessed teams of seven Clydesdales to plow the prairies of Australia, Canada, and the United States.

appaloosa
toponym: Palouse River, Oregon

The American Appaloosa was first bred by a Native American people called the Nez Percé. Using stock from the sixteenth-century Spanish conquistadores, they called the horse the Palouse, after their tribal lands around the Palouse River in Oregon. The word *Appaloosa* grew out of the original Palouse.

Expert horse breeders, the Nez Percé wanted a practical, hardy mount for hunting and defending their land. They bred for a short, sparse mane and tail since long, flowing hair could easily get tangled in bushes. The classic Appaloosa's coat is always spotted, either in a marbleized or leopard pattern.

morgan

eponym: Justin Morgan

Today nobody would dream of hitching up a team of Morgans to pull a heavy wagon. With their characteristic exaggerated high-stepping gait and long, flowing tail brushing the ground, these small, delicate horses are favorites in equestrian show rings.

All Morgans trace their heritage back to one magnificent dark bay stallion named Justin Morgan. Born in either 1789 or 1793, in West Springfield, Massachusetts, the horse's original name was Figure. In 1795, Figure was bought by a Vermont schoolteacher and innkeeper named Justin Morgan, and the horse was given his master's name. In Vermont, Morgan used his new horse for plowing and clearing woods, and in competitive hauling matches and races. The animal's stamina became legendary. The horse died in 1821 with a perfect, unbeaten record.

The United States Cavalry often chose the powerful, strong-hearted Morgans, despite their compact size, as their preferred mount during the 1800s.

bantam

toponym: Bantam, Java

Nearly four hundred years ago representatives of the Dutch East India Company set up trading offices in the territory of Bantam, on the Pacific island of Java. There they found a small domestic chicken that was given the name bantam from the area, which is now known as Banten.

Bantams are considered miniature chickens since most weigh less than one and a half pounds. Although some people raise bantams for their small eggs, the chickens are most often kept as a hobby for exhibition in poultry shows.

Bantam is also a term referring to anything that is light in weight. For example, a boxer competing in the bantamweight division must weigh in at between 112 and 118 pounds before the match. Only flyweights, boxers under 112 pounds, are lighter.

holstein

toponym: Schleswig-Holstein, Germany

If you ever went to a country fair or visited a dairy farm, you probably remember seeing cows with a very distinctive splotchy black-and-white pattern on their bodies. The full name for this dairy cow with the familiar coat is holstein-friesian. Not all holsteins, however, have black-and-white coats. Some are red and white, while others are nearly solid black or white.

From what we know, the cattle were developed from stock that came from the province of Friesland in the Netherlands. Cattle breeders in the state of Schleswig-Holstein, Germany, also had a hand in perfecting the breed, so the name was hyphenated to represent both areas.

Introduced into the United States in 1795, holsteins make up the largest population of dairy cows in the country. They owe most of their popularity to their efficiency as milk producers, with an average annual yield of 14,000 pounds of milk per cow.

guernsey   **toponym: Guernsey, Channel Islands, England**

Cattle breeders on the island of Guernsey took red-streaked cattle from Normandy, in northwestern France, and bred them with the smaller brown-and-white cattle from the neighboring region of Brittany. The resulting cow was fawn-colored with white markings and a yellow skin.

Introduced into the United States in 1831, several years after the holstein, guernseys are a favorite with farmers who want milk with a higher fat content, or butterfat, than holsteins produce. Butterfat rises to the top in containers of all raw milk after it has set, and is used to make butter.

a rhinestone romance

romance

toponym: Rome, Italy

In the 1950s several romantic movies were set in Rome, among them *Roman Holiday* and *Three Coins in the Fountain*. And to understand the origins of the word *romance,* we, too, must visit Rome.

In its original meaning *romance* had nothing to do with couples pairing off. It referred to the languages like French, Spanish, and Italian that descended from Latin as spoken by the Romans. Later, *romance* came to mean a long fictional piece marked by sweeping adventures and daring heroes. The notion of romantic love most likely arose out of those stories of chivalry because such bravery was admirable—and desirable!

Now juicy romance novels fill book racks everywhere. Some people read them to escape to another land—perhaps even Rome.

serendipity

eponym: The Three Princes of Serendip
toponym: Serendib (Sri Lanka)

Imagine that a year after your best friend moves hundreds of miles away, you bump into each other during summer vacation. What a delightful surprise! You could also call the chance meeting serendipitous.

In an old Persian fairy tale titled *The Three Princes of Serendip,* three journeying princes meet with wonderful surprises along the way. When English writer Horace Walpole retold the fairy tale in 1754, he didn't realize he had

coined a new word. Borrowing its name from the princes' homeland, *serendipity* came to mean the ability to find unexpected good fortune.

chantilly

Brides often wear gowns and veils embellished with lace. Thousands of miles west of fictional Serendip lies the small town of Chantilly, France. In the nineteenth century, Chantilly was famous the world over for its manufacture of an especially beautiful lace called Chantilly. Still produced today, Chantilly lace features a delicate floral or scrolled design in its cobweblike mesh. Maybe you have heard a classic rock-and-roll hit from the 1950s called "Chantilly Lace."

Chantilly also gave its name to another frilly concoction, a cream topping that is piped in a lacy pattern on typically rich French desserts.

rhinestone

toponym: Rhine River, Germany

Most lovers would probably consider rhinestones a cheap substitute for the real thing, a brilliant, costly diamond. The story behind the word *rhinestone* is set in Germany, along the Rhine River. Over a hundred years ago, sparkling, clear rocks were first mined there and cut to look like diamonds.

Since a rhinestone refers to a fake diamond, the word *rhinestone* is sometimes applied to people or objects that aren't the real thing, such as a rhinestone cowboy.

turquoise

toponym: Turkey

Those readers born in December may be familiar with turquoise, the birthstone for the twelfth month. The sky blue semiprecious gem has been used ornamentally for over 5,000 years and was a special favorite among the ancient Egyptians.

In modern times, the first turquoise was shipped to Europe from Turkey. Because of this association with Turkey, the stone was called *turquoyse* in Middle French, and later turquoise. Today, deposits of the blue to bluish green mineral are mined throughout the world, in Arizona, Nevada, Iran, and yes, even Turkey.

cologne
toponym: Köln (Cologne in French), Germany

Maybe you'd rather get a bottle of your favorite cologne for your December birthday. Cologne borrowed its name from Köln, Germany, an ancient city first settled by the Romans.

The first perfumes arrived in Europe 800 years ago, but cologne is a younger scent relative. Cologne was the sweet-smelling invention of a French barber, who mixed together oils, bitters, and ethyl alcohol in Cologne in 1709. The mixture was called in French *eau de Cologne,* "water of Cologne." Now the term *cologne* is generally applied to fragrances from many different regions.

Why does perfume cost a lot more than cologne? By law perfume must contain at least 25 percent perfume oils, while colognes are only 3 to 5 percent oils.

sideburns
eponym: Ambrose Burnside

Male facial hair has gone in and out of fashion for thousands of years. From archaeological digs we know that the cavemen got a close shave with razors made of sharpened flints and seashells. Upper-class Greek men were also always clean shaven.

In contrast, judging from paintings and photographs of nineteenth-century presidents, beards were definitely all the rage. And so were sideburns, thanks to an American Civil War general named Ambrose Burnside. The general's whiskers, which crept far out onto his cheeks, were first called burnsides after their creator. Then, for reasons unknown, someone rearranged *burnsides* to *sideburns.*

When a new word is formed by rearranging the letters of another word it's called an anagram. *Sideburns* may be the only eponym that's also an anagram. Or perhaps you can think of another.

cashmere
toponym: Kashmir, India

Like angora, cashmere is a soft, valuable fabric used to make expensive clothing. And like angora, cashmere gets its name from an actual place, making it a toponym.

Cashmere is the English spelling for Kashmir, a state in northern India. There, high in the rocky Himalayas, lives an animal called the cashmere goat. The top layer of the cashmere goat's coat is coarse, but the undercoat is soft and downy. It's this fluffy undercoat that is used to manufacture cashmere. Cashmere is so costly because one goat yields only around three ounces of undercoat a year.

silhouette

Did you ever cut out the shape of a person or animal from black paper and mount it on a light background? Or maybe you've held your fingers against a wall to make a shadow picture. This dark outline is called a silhouette. Before modern photography, many courting couples exchanged silhouette profiles of one another.

We know that the word *silhouette* came from Étienne de Silhouette, the minister of finance for French king Louis XV. But no one really knows why. Some historians think it's because the minister collected outline portraits, which were then named after him. Others suggest that because of Silhouette's unpopularity at court his enemies used his name to describe a shadowlike lack of substance.

pompadour
eponym: Marquise de Pompadour

Étienne de Silhouette was booted out of the court of Louis XV within a year. But the king's steady companion, Jeanne-Antoinette Poisson, influenced his decisions in matters of state for many years. To show his gratitude, Louis gave her a posh estate called Pompadour, from which she got her more popular name, Madame de Pompadour.

What the king's paramour is best remembered for, however, is not her role as foreign affairs adviser but her hairstyle. The marquise liked to brush her hair in a series of coils that outlined her face like a picture frame.

When a man mounds his hair up in the front, like a 1950s rock star, and slathers on a lot of goopy gel to keep it in place, he's sporting what's known as a pompadour.

limousine
toponym: Limousin Province, France

The long, luxurious VIP-mobile got its name from a province in central France called Limousin. But it wasn't because, as you might think, limousines were first built there.

It happened this way. A few hundred years ago, French herdsmen in Limousin kept warm and dry by wearing a protective outfit with a hood called a *limousine*. Since the cloak was named a limousine after Limousin province, it's a toponym.

In the early 1900s in France, an enclosed horse-drawn coach, with a hoodlike roof that protected the driver, also became known as a limousine. This was probably because someone thought the covered front compartment on the carriage looked like the garment's hood. From the horse-drawn coach we get the name for our luxury coach.

dollar
toponym: Joachimstaler, Bohemia

We all know people need dollars to buy limos and cashmere. But the tongue twister *Joachimstaler* sounds very different from the word *dollar,* which is one of the few words in English with a Bohemian background.

In 1519, an aristocratic family in Joachimsthal, Bohemia (now in the newly formed Czech Republic), minted coins from their own silver mine. Because the family lived in St. Joachim, the coins were called Joachimstalers, which became shortened, mercifully, to *talers.*

The Dutch later turned *taler* into *daler.* Later still, the English converted *daler* to *dollar*, and the word for our monetary unit was born, thanks to a silver mine thousands of miles away.

italic

Did you notice that several of the foreign words in the last entry looked different from the rest? They were printed in italics. The letters of italic words slant upward to the right, *like this*. Foreign words and

words that the writer wants to emphasize are printed in italics.

The word *italic* came directly from Italy, specifically from a Venetian printer who, in 1501, printed a book in this slanted-type style. The type was called *Italicus,* later anglicized to *italic*.

valentine

One of the most popular names associated with romance is Valentine. It gets a little confusing since there were actually two men named Valentine, a Roman bishop and a priest, who were both executed for their religious beliefs in the late third century. These two Valentines died a few years apart, on February 14, after which both men became saints.

But what do martyred Christians have in common with our most romantic holiday? Some say Bishop Valentine was jailed for marrying couples in secret; others claim he, himself, fell in love with the jailer's blind daughter and wrote letters to her signed, what else, "from your Valentine."

The most believable explanation is that the Catholic Church converted a midwinter Roman pagan celebration, which included couples pairing off, to a feast day that commemorated the day both Valentines died, February 14. They called this feast day Saint Valentine's Day.

gypsy

toponym: Egypt

 Valentine's Day dinner with a strolling gypsy violinist—sound romantic? Many people think it does, which is why some restaurants hire violinists dressed in colorful outfits.

We now know that the people known as Gypsies trace their beginnings to India. As early as the fourteenth century, they left India for Europe, where they wandered from place to place. Yet because these people have dark skin and hair similar to Egyptians, it was mistakenly assumed that they came from Egypt. Based on this wrong assumption, these Indians were given the name Gypsy, an abbreviation of *Egyptian*.

chauvinist

eponym: Nicholas Chauvin

One way of criticizing a man who exhibits feelings of superiority to the opposite sex is to call him a male chauvinist. But the story of how the word came into being had nothing at all to do with the sexes.

Nicholas Chauvin was a soldier who served in Napoléon Bonaparte's army in the early nineteenth century. So dedicated was Chauvin to Napoléon and to France that his fellow soldiers made fun of his unquestioning devotion.

Because of Chauvin's unflagging loyalty, the term *chauvinist* was applied to anyone who was extremely patriotic. The meaning later expanded to include people with strong feelings about any group or place. Nowadays, however, we mostly hear about chauvinists and chauvinism during discussions of male-female relationships.

echo
narcissist

**eponym: Echo, Greek nymph
Narcissus, Greek boy**

Picture this: someone is walking through the mountains calling out, "I love me most of all." Seconds later "I love me most of all," echoes back to the caller. One particular story in Greek mythology gives us the clues behind the terms for both reflected sounds, called *echoes,* and *narcissists,* people who think the world of themselves.

A woodland nymph named Echo desperately loved the handsome youth Narcissus. But Narcissus didn't even know Echo was alive. Sick at heart, the maiden pined away from her unrequited love for Narcissus, until nothing remained but Echo's voice.

But Echo got even with Narcissus when she made him fall in love with his own reflection in a pool. Staring intently and admiringly into the water, the Greek youth, too, pined away and was changed into a narcissus flower, a kind of daffodil.

tangerines and tootsie rolls

fig newton
toponym: Newton, Massachusetts

Over a hundred years ago the first fig-filled cookie rolled off the production line at the Kennedy Biscuit Works in Cambridge, Massachusetts. The cookie makers wanted to name their new chewy sweet after a local town, but they agreed that Fig Cambridge was a real mouthful. Fig Boston didn't get many votes, either. Then a factory employee from nearby Newton nominated his hometown. The decision was unanimous: *Fig Newton* had a real ring to it.

It's amazing but true. Americans eat more than 65 million pounds of Fig Newton cookies every year. After Chips Ahoy! and Oreos, Fig Newtons are this country's best-selling cookie.

bologna
toponym: Bologna, Italy

Nobody has ever stopped to add up how many bologna sandwiches are eaten every year. But we do know the favorite lunch meat got its name from Bologna, a city and province in central Italy. The original sausages made in Bologna were stuffed with leftovers of all sorts, mixed together with spicy seasonings. Today most bologna in this country is sold as processed cold cuts.

Baloney is the American slang spelling of bologna. Did you ever hear anyone say "baloney" when referring to something that's worthless or doesn't make sense? The word may have acquired this meaning because the early Italian bologna sausages contained leftovers that weren't worth much. And that's no phony-baloney!

frankfurter

Although cooks have been stuffing leftover meats and spices into casings for thousands of years, we can only guess who shaped the first sausage. The Greeks, the Romans, and the Babylonians are all good candidates.

The word *frankfurter,* however, can be traced directly to Frankfurt, Germany. In the 1850s, Frankfurt butchers introduced a slightly curved sausage they named the frankfurter, after their hometown. According to a popular story, a butcher's low-slung pet dachshund inspired the shape. The sausage was a big hit, and 30 years later German immigrants in the United States started cranking them out.

Americans eat about 17 billion frankfurters a year. In 1916 franks sold for a nickel at Nathan's hot dog concession in Coney Island, New York. In some areas of the country, in fact, frankfurters are called Coney Islands. Nathan's still grills franks, but the price has gone up to almost two dollars.

hot dog Although *hot dog* isn't technically an eponym or a toponym, the story behind the word is interesting enough to merit a detour.

By the time the frankfurter migrated to America in the 1880s, it was already nicknamed "hot dachshund." Then, in 1906, a New York cartoonist drew a cartoon of a dachshund dog sandwiched between a bun. When the artist had trouble spelling *dachshund,* he abbreviated the caption to "hot dog." Whether fact or fiction (the original cartoon was never found), it makes for a hot dog of a story. "Get your hot dachshund!" doesn't quite cut the mustard, does it?

hamburger   **toponym: Hamburg, Germany**

Hamburgers and their grill relatives, hot dogs, both share the same toponymous source—Germany. The beef patty's history is even older.

More than six centuries ago, a warlike Russian tribe called the Tartars passed on a culinary tip to the Germans: in order to make poor-quality beef taste better, shred it and add spices. When this dish was prepared in Hamburg, raw or cooked, it was labeled Hamburg steak.

In the 1880s—about the same time the frankfurter was making its debut—the hamburg steak was introduced in the United States as the hamburger. Restaurants at the 1904 Saint Louis World's Fair served hamburgers in buns. There, gentlemen in their best suits may have also worn a felt hat with a firm brim called a homburg, after another city in Germany, Homburg. Do homburg wearers prefer to eat hamburgers or frankfurters?

Guess which fast-food restaurant chain sold the first hamburger? No, not McDonald's. It was White Castle.

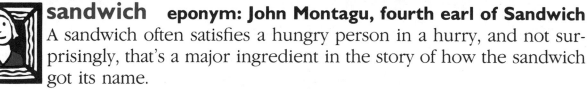

sandwich   eponym: John Montagu, fourth earl of Sandwich

A sandwich often satisfies a hungry person in a hurry, and not surprisingly, that's a major ingredient in the story of how the sandwich got its name.

John Montagu, the earl of Sandwich, was so addicted to gambling he wouldn't leave the gaming tables, even to eat. One day in the 1760s, a hungry John Montagu had someone bring him meat and cheese stuffed between two pieces of bread. This suited the earl perfectly since he didn't have to stop playing in order to eat. He held the sandwich in one hand and played blackjack with the other.

Did you know the Hawaiian Islands were first called the Sandwich Islands, after the earl of Sandwich, who was First Lord of the Admiralty when Captain Cook discovered the islands?

42

hoagie
toponym: Hog Island, Pennsylvania

His lordship, the earl, might have had a harder time playing blackjack with a hoagie in one hand. A hoagie is a long sandwich stuffed with a variety of meats, cheeses, and garnishes. Depending on where you live, it's also called a hero, grinder, submarine, or poor boy.

In word history terms, *hoagie* is a new kid on the block, coming into use only in the last twenty-five years. And although its history is a little fuzzy, there's a very good possibility that *hoagie* is another edible toponym.

The stretch sandwich was probably named for Hog Island, a small island on the Delaware River near Philadelphia. There, hungry ship workers feasted on lunchtime sandwiches served on a long roll. These meal-sized sandwiches were first called Hog Island sandwiches and, later, hoagies.

mayonnaise
toponym: Mahón, Spain

Today we slather mayonnaise on sandwiches, but when the zesty sauce was first invented it was designed for the best cuts of dinnertime meat. It was on the Spanish island of Minorca that someone first blended together oil, lemon juice, egg yolk, and seasonings. Since the sauce was created in the port city of Mahón, it became known as mayonnaise.

Mayonnaise's place of origin is undisputed. Yet both the French and Spanish boast they invented the dressing. According to the Spanish version, an unnamed farmer's wife first mixed up the ingredients. The French—famous for sauces like hollandaise and bernaise—claim mayonnaise was the creation of the duc de Richelieu's personal chef.

french fry
toponym: France

For three decades french fries have been a winning course in a fast-food meal, especially with youngsters. But the crispy fries go back at least three hundred years.

It was then that the French began to cut up potatoes into thick slices and fry them. In those days french fried potatoes were on the menu at elegant state dinners. One of the earliest fans of these thick-cut potatoes was Thomas Jefferson, who sampled them while America's ambassador to France. Ambassador Jefferson brought back the recipe for french fried potatoes in order to serve them to his dinner guests at Monticello. *French fried potatoes* was abbreviated to *french fries* around 1918.

turkey

Were turkeys named after the country we associate with steam baths, coffee, and richly colored carpets? Yes, but it was all a case of mistaken identity.

Guinea fowl are birds that don't look at all like our turkeys. They're much smaller and have short necks, featherless heads, and dark bodies speckled with white feathers. Yet when a load of guinea fowl was transported through the Turkish Empire en route to Europe, no one recognized them as guinea fowl. As a result, they were called turkeys, since they had a stopover in Turkey.

A short time later, sixteenth-century Spanish explorers carried a large flightless bird with a long neck from South America back to Europe. When it arrived, someone thought this bird, which looked like our modern Thanksgiving bird, resembled the guinea fowl (the ones already mislabeled as turkeys), so the long-necked bird was also called a turkey.

One error compounded another. Eventually, guinea fowl were correctly identified, but the South American bird kept the name turkey. And turkey it will probably remain for countless Thanksgivings to come.

tangerine

toponym: Tangier, Morocco

The 1940s movie classic *Casablanca* took place in the exotic Moroccan city of the same name. Tangier, another seaport city in Morocco, is the place where the tasty, easy-to-peel tangerine originated.

After the orange, the tangerine is the second most economically important citrus fruit in the world. It's called a tangerine because it was exported to Europe via Tangier in the 1840s. In fact, the fragrant fruit was originally called a Tangiers orange, before its name changed to tangerine.

mcintosh apple

eponym: John McIntosh

What does a disappointing love affair have to do with the first McIntosh tree? After quarreling with his parents over a woman, John McIntosh left home in 1776 with a broken heart and settled in the Saint Lawrence Valley, in Ontario, Canada.

It was there on his farm that McIntosh first grew the apples named after him. His son William went on to develop a nursery and then traveled by horse and wagon throughout northern New York and Vermont peddling the trees. With its sweet perfume and aroma, the McIntosh remains a prized eating, baking, and cider-making apple.

seltzer

toponym: Selters, Germany

What are you drinking with your sandwich, a soft drink or maybe clear, sparkling water called seltzer?

Fizzy seltzer is produced artificially by filtering and carbonating mineral water. But when seltzer was first discovered in the mid-1700s it occurred naturally in springs near a village called Selters. The effervescent liquid was first called Selters water, then later seltzer.

hershey bar

eponym: Milton Hershey

Up until 1900 only the upper class could afford to buy costly chocolate. Enter candy maker Milton Hershey with a dream: to make chocolate the general public could enjoy. So after selling his Lancaster, Pennsylvania, caramel factory, Hershey imported a German chocolate-making machine and got busy mixing together sugar, cocoa, chocolate, and milk.

The sweet results came in 1903, with the famous nickel candy bar that carried Milton Hershey's name. When the public's sweet tooth demanded more, Hershey built the country's largest chocolate-manufacturing plant near Harrisburg. He developed an entire community, called Hershey, around the plant, where his workers could live with their families.

tootsie roll

eponym: Clara Hirschfield

A couple of years after the first Hershey bar melted in someone's pocket, another candy maker came up with a recipe for a candy bar with a distinct advantage: it wouldn't melt in your pocket or purse. This was a revolutionary turn in the pre-M&M's candy-making industry.

The man responsible for the chewy Tootsie Roll was candy maker Leonard Hirschfield. Hirschfield, a young man in his twenties when he invented the candy bar, decided to name the sweet after his young daughter, Clara, nicknamed "Tootsie."

baby ruth

eponym: Ruth Cleveland

A presidential daughter is behind the Baby Ruth candy bar, a yummy confection of chocolate, peanuts, and caramel, introduced in 1921. The baby in the candy bar's name was actually Ruth Cleveland, infant daughter of Grover Cleveland, this country's 22d and 24th president.

Many people mistakenly think the eponym behind the Baby Ruth is Babe Ruth, the famous baseball slugger of the 1920s. Although the famous home-run hitter had no part in the naming of the Baby Ruth, candy bars like the Baby Ruth scored a big hit with baseball fans in stadiums across the country. Thanks to sales at game concessions, candy bars soon became an American institution.

toponym: Milky Way galaxy
Far from the lights of a city, look up at the sky on a clear night. If the moon isn't full, you might see a hazy white band stretching across the ink-blue sky. This band, called the Milky Way, is caused by light from many faint stars.

We know the galaxy inspired the name for the Milky Way candy bar—but why? Perhaps its creator, Franklin Mars, wanted people to think the candy bar's mixture of chocolate, milk, butter, and malt was a heavenly combination. Or maybe it was because Mars's last name is also the name of the red planet. Whatever the reason, the candy bar made Mars a confectionery star in the 1920s. Later he added Snickers, 3 Musketeers, and M&M's to his candy-bar galaxy.

CANDY

toll house cookie

toponym: Toll House Inn, Whitman, Massachusetts

The story behind the name of the first chocolate chip cookie goes back 300 years. Then, horse-drawn coaches traveling between Boston and New Bedford, Massachusetts, stopped halfway in the town of Whitman to pay a toll at a tollhouse. In the 1920s, a local woman named Ruth Wakefield restored the old tollhouse and opened it as the Toll House Inn.

Ten years later while the innkeeper, a noted baker, was mixing up a batch of butter cookies, she decided to toss a few chunks of semisweet chocolate into the batter. The experiment drew four-star reviews from her guests.

In 1939 the Nestlé Company began to package ready-to-use real chocolate morsels especially designed for chocolate chip cookies. Nestlé also bought the rights to print Ruth Wakefield's original cookie recipe on the label. It's still there.

walnut

eponym: Wales (Welsh)

When you make chocolate chip cookies do you add nuts to the batter? If so, maybe you use walnuts. In word history, *walnut* evolved from *Welsh,* the word for people who live in Wales, in the United Kingdom. But the oily nuts are native to what was ancient Persia. How, then, did *Welsh* get into the nut-naming picture?

When the Persian walnut first arrived in England via Europe over eleven centuries ago, the English called it a *wealhhnutu,* which translates as "Welsh nut." Since the Welsh were Celtic people who migrated from southeastern Gaul (now France), they were considered foreigners by the English. The English, who had a habit of poking fun at anything foreign, did so by calling it Welsh. *Wealhhnutu* later became *walnot,* then *walnut.*

fudge

eponym: Captain Fudge

Toss some walnuts into a mixture of milk, sugar, butter, and flavorings and you get walnut fudge. The first pan of fudge hardened around 1896. The phrase *to fudge* is much older and may refer to a real person.

In correspondence from the 1660s we know that a man named Captain Fudge served in Her Majesty's Royal Navy. In fact, in some parts of England today Fudge is still a common last name. It seems that Captain Fudge had a reputation for stretching the truth. So when sailors cried out "Just fudge it," they were referring to the tall tales told by their captain. Did you ever fudge it by fibbing about who really ate the last piece of walnut fudge?

currant   toponym: Corinth, Greece

Today fewer than 25,000 people live in the Greek port city of Corinth. But 2,000 years ago Corinth was a bustling city with a population of over one million residents. Corinth is best remembered for two things that still carry its name: the Corinthian column with its ornate, scrolled, bell-shaped top, and a tasty seedless raisin called the Corinth grape.

So popular were these small seedless raisins that they were exported all over the world. In English the name became currant.

graham cracker

eponym: Sylvester Graham

Sylvester Graham may have been one of America's first health-food gurus. More than 170 years ago Graham was advising people to eat a low-fat, high-carbohydrate diet and exercise regularly. And Sylvester Graham practiced what he preached. Disciples clustered around the Connecticut-based, self-proclaimed "reverend" and "doctor." Despite his healthy lifestyle, Sylvester Graham died at the age of 57 of tuberculosis.

One of Graham's biggest taboos was white flour. Out of his health-conscious teachings came whole wheat products like Graham crackers. Although the crispy crackers aren't usually considered health food, they're a less sugary snack than cookies or candy. Unless, of course, you combine the crackers with marshmallows and chocolate into a lip-smacking gooey treat sometimes called s'mores (slang for "some more"). Can you guess how they got their name?

melba toast

eponym: Nellie Melba

Had he lived another 60 years, Sylvester Graham would certainly have put his stamp of approval on the thin, dry toast called melba.

The woman who inspired the name of the dry toast was a much-loved opera singer named Nellie Melba, who fought the scales all her life. To give the singer something low calorie to munch on with her morning tea, the famous French chef Auguste Escoffier sliced bread as thinly as possible and toasted it. Melba loved it—or said she did—and several years later it was packaged for general use.

Chef Escoffier, however, tipped the diet scales against the soprano when, in 1892, he concocted peach melba—a sinful blend of ice cream, peaches, and raspberry sauce—in the diva's honor.

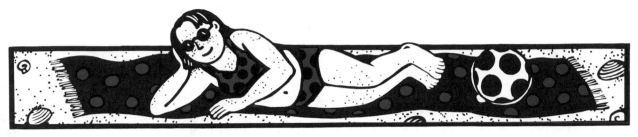

a polka-dot bikini

leotard
eponym: Jules Léotard

Do you know the song "The Daring Young Man on the Flying Trapeze"? The first line goes: "He flies through the air with the greatest of ease." The adventurous young man in the song was French trapeze artist Jules Léotard. And it was this same acrobat who gave his name to the thin, clinging garment called the leotard.

When Jules Léotard performed his airborne somersaults in the mid-1800s he wanted to wear a garment that wouldn't interfere with his flips and spins. So the artist designed a close-fitting costume that became known as the leotard. Dressed in the skimpy, skintight outfit, the acrobat's leotard got as many oohs and ahhs as his high-flying act. Today, the eponymous leotard is worn for dancing, gymnastics, exercising—and, of course, trapeze flying.

levi's
eponym: Levi Strauss

Have you ever worn a pair of Levi's blue jeans? The man behind these pants was garment merchant Levi Strauss. Strauss started out in the 1850s making tents and wagons out of canvas during the California gold rush, which peaked in 1852. Then the tailor switched to sewing canvas overalls. Because the stiff pants were so sturdy and lasted a long time they were bought up by prospectors mining for gold.

denim
toponym: Nîmes, France

After first producing work pants out of rough canvas, Levi Strauss switched to a fabric that was softer than canvas but just as strong. The fabric, woven in Nîmes, France, was called *serge de Nîmes,* "serge from Nîmes."

In the United States, *serge de Nîmes* was shortened and anglicized to *denim.* Levi Strauss dyed the sturdy serge a dark blue color to help hide dirt and stains. From the late 1860s on, Levi's denim blue jeans became the standard dress for hard-working cowboys and miners in the Old West.

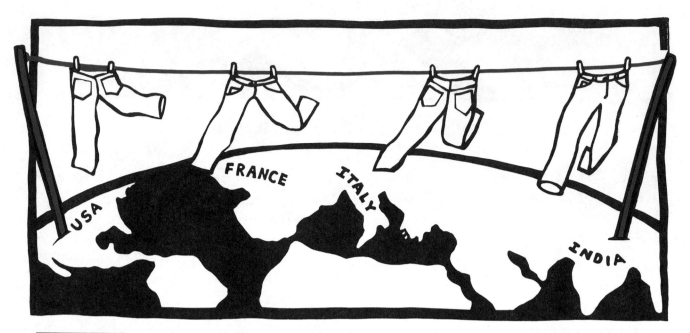

jeans

toponym: Genoa, Italy

Blue jeans are as American as apple pie. The outfit of the cowboys and miners became a hot American fashion item in the 1930s. But, as we read, denim came from France. And the word *jean* originated in Genoa, Italy.

Over a hundred years ago, French weavers crossed the Italian border to work at fabric mills in Genoa. The French nickname for Genoa was "Gene." At the mills, the weavers made a strong cotton fabric, similar to *serge de Nîmes,* which was used to make work clothing. When this fabric was exported to the United States, *gene* was Americanized to *jean,* giving American blue jeans a dual French-Italian passport.

dungaree

toponym: Dongri Killa, India

We know that denim originated in Nîmes, France, while jeans have their fabric roots in Genoa, Italy. Another name for jeans is dungarees. In order to unravel the story behind *dungarees,* we must travel from Europe to Asia, specifically to India.

The most widely spoken language in northern India is Hindi. *Dungaree* is the Americanized version of the Hindi word *dungri,* which refers to a coarse, inexpensive cotton. The cloth was called dungri because it was sold around Dongri Killa, which in English refers to the Fort George district in the city of Bombay.

stetson

eponym: John B. Stetson

While Levi Strauss was busy outfitting the western cowboys in tough denim pants, Philadelphia hatmaker John B. Stetson came up with a design for a ten-gallon hat that became their official headgear.

While Stetson was vacationing in the Midwest during the 1860s, he met cattle ranchers who expressed interest in a hat that would protect them from the sun and elements but was also stylish. Back in Philadelphia, Stetson came up with an oversized hat expressly for these ranchers. The hat was an overnight success, and before long the Stetson was as much a part of a cowboy as his horse. Both Annie Oakley and Buffalo Bill wore custom-made Stetsons.

jodhpur

toponym: Jodhpur, India

Not everyone who goes horseback riding puts on a pair of blue jeans and a cowboy hat. Some equestrians wear helmets and tight-fitting riding pants that flare out at the thigh. The story behind how these pants got their name is set in India.

Two centuries ago, men in northwestern India wore cotton flared pants as part of their everyday dress. They lived in a town and district called Jodhpur, now in Rajasthan. During the 200 years of British rule in India, British horse enthusiasts turned the cotton pants into riding breeches by adding a foot strap. The trousers, which became known as jodhpurs, traveled back to England, where they were all the rage.

calico

toponym: Calicut, India

Like *jodhpur,* the word *calico* has an Indian background. In the sixteenth century, Calicut was one of the major Indian ports trading between India and Europe, located on the Malabar coast. Calicut's chief export was a fine cotton, which became known as calico. Originally calico was the general name applied to all plain cotton from the East. Later, calico was brightly dyed and printed with the variegated patterns so popular today.

Have you ever seen a cat with a blotchy black, white, and orange coat? These cats, called calicos, are unusual in another way: they're almost always female.

knickers

eponym: Diedrich Knickerbocker

When the Dutch came to America in the seventeenth century, a common last name among these immigrants was Knickerbocker. American writer Washington Irving invented a character called Diedrich Knickerbocker for his 1809 satirical book, entitled *A History of New York from the Beginning of the World to the End of the Dutch Dynasty*. After publication, the name Knickerbocker became an expression to describe anyone who came from Holland.

The Dutch wore loose-fitting pants that were gathered, and sometimes buckled, at the knee. Within a short time, young American boys began to wear these short pants, which became known as knickers, short for the surname Knickerbocker. So out of a long-winded title came a shortened name for a short pair of pants.

bloomers

eponym: Amelia Bloomer

We have a woman to thank for making another pair of loose-fitting pants so famous that her name became part of our vocabulary. Amelia Bloomer, an early advocate of women's rights in the mid-1800s, was also a fashion rebel. Instead of wearing the typical hoopskirts and crinolines of her day, Amelia dressed in baggy pants and a short tunic.

Other women campaigning for the right to vote copied Mrs. Bloomer's uniform, and before long bloomers symbolized feminist rebellion. Bloomers also made good practical sense, particularly for bicycle riding, since long skirts often got caught up in the bike's chain mechanism and even the wheels.

chartreuse
toponym: La Grande Chartreuse, France

Some of you may use a bright greenish yellow chartreuse felt-tip marker for highlighting lines in a book when you are studying. The toponym source of the color chartreuse is La Grande Chartreuse monastery, located in the Alps of southeastern France.

In 1607 the monks at La Grande Chartreuse began producing a clear, greenish yellow liqueur from the root of the angelica plant. Because the liqueur—which is still sold today—was produced at La Grande Chartreuse monastery, it became known as Chartreuse. The name of the liqueur is spelled with a capital *C,* but chartreuse with a lowercase *c* refers to the neon-bright greenish color.

magenta
eponym: Marcus Maxentius
toponym: Magenta, Italy

Chartreuse and magenta are two very popular fashion colors, used to dye everything from sweat suits to sofas. *Magenta* has an especially fascinating word history. Evolving over a span of 16 centuries, the word was first a general's name, then a town's name, then a brilliant reddish purple color.

When the Roman general Marcus Maxentius stationed his troops in a small town near Milan in the fourth century, the town was named Magenta in his honor. Fifteen centuries later, a bright purplish red dye was developed in Magenta. Named after the town, which was, in turn, named after the Roman general, magenta was the first chemical dye ever used to color material for garments.

bikini
toponym: Bikini Atoll

At first look, it doesn't seem at all surprising that a coral island called the Bikini Atoll inspired the name for the itsy-bitsy bikini bathing suit. After all, bikinis and tropical islands have always gone hand in hand. But there's more to the story.

In the summer of 1946, a Parisian fashion designer named Louis Réard was about to reveal his newest creation, a revealing two-piece swimsuit, at a Paris fashion show. But the designer needed a name for his bathing suit. During this time the United States, as part of its peacetime nuclear testing, dropped an atomic bomb on the Bikini Atoll in the Pacific's Marshall Islands. So Louis Réard simply borrowed the word *bikini* from the latest newspaper headlines and dropped a fashion bomb of his own.

paisley

The curvy paisley pattern found in fabrics today gets its name from Paisley, Scotland, a city near Glasgow. For many years Paisley was a center of weaving and thread manufacturing.

When the European demand for cashmere shawls peaked in the nineteenth century, the Paisley weavers produced a less expensive copy. In the process, they wove a distinctive wavy pattern into the wool, which became known as paisley. Today paisley patterns are incorporated into all kinds of fabric, from cotton to cashmere.

polka dot toponym: Poland (Polish)

The polka is a lively dance with short half-steps in 2/4 time, which was first danced in Bohemia, now part of the Czech Republic. Bands with accordion players usually accompany people dancing the polka. In the Polish language, *Polka* means "Polish woman," the feminine of *Polak,*

"Pole." After the polka became all the rage in 1900, its name was tacked onto a wide variety of things. These included polka gauze, a polka hat, and, the most familiar, the polka dot. The polka-dot pattern continues to be one of the most popular fabric designs.

suede toponym: Sweden

If you've ever rubbed your fingers over something made of suede, you know that it's very soft to the touch. Ironically, the softness of suede is produced when leather is buffed against a rough wheel. This raises a soft nap and gives the fabric or skin a luxuriously velvety texture.

Over a century ago, glovemakers in Sweden used skins with this soft nap to make fine gloves, which were then exported. The fashionable gloves were especially in demand in France, where they were called *gants de Suède,* or "gloves of Sweden." The toponymous name stuck. Nowadays any leather or cloth that is treated to raise a soft nap is called suede.

tuxedo

toponym: Tuxedo Park, New York

Throughout most of the 1800s, proper formal dress for a man included a coat with long tails and a black tie. That all changed in 1886 in Tuxedo, New York, when tobacco heir Griswold Lorillard and his friends showed up at the Tuxedo Club decked out in scarlet vests and black dinner jackets. The scarlet vests didn't shock guests at the posh club, but dinner jackets without tails raised society eyebrows.

Why young Lorillard asked his tailor to omit the tails is not clear. He may have gotten the idea from the tailless riding jackets favored by English equestrians. Or perhaps he was influenced by the comfort-loving English king, Edward VII, who, suffering from the heat during a trip to India, wore a tailless coat.

galosh

toponym: Gaul

To find the toponym source for *galosh* we must go back to an ancient country in western Europe called Gaul, now part of France, Belgium, and northern Italy. On a typical rainy day in Gaul, people protected their cloth shoes by covering them with wooden sandals laced up to midcalf.

The name for these shoes, *gallica solea,* or "Gaulish shoes," was compressed and anglicized over the centuries to our present word, *galosh.* The raised wooden sandals offered some protection from the rain and snow. However it wasn't until nearly two thousand years later that people were able to keep their feet completely dry in a downpour.

mackintosh

eponym: Charles Macintosh

The man who did the most to help people keep dry in the rain was born in a country famous for its "liquid sunshine." The Scotsman's name was Charles Macintosh, an industrial chemist and inventor.

In June 1823 Macintosh discovered a process in which he was able to waterproof material by sandwiching rubber between two layers of wool. The bulky waterproof rubber raincoats that were manufactured some seven years later were named in honor of Charles Macintosh, the chemist who invented the revolutionary process. Today, especially in England, the raincoat is often referred to as a mac.

hyacinth

eponym: Hyacinthus, Greek youth

Zephyrus may have saved the day for poor abandoned Psyche, but once provoked, Zephyrus could also use his winds destructively. One day, as the Greek god of light, Apollo, was about to throw a discus, a jealous Zephyrus used his wind to spoil Apollo's aim. As a result, the hurtling discus struck Apollo's friend Hyacinthus and killed him.

According to the legend, a beautiful flower sprang up on the very spot where Hyacinthus's blood stained the ground. A deep purple lily-shaped flower, the hyacinth in the legend is not the same fragrant spiky spring flower we grow today from bulbs.

ocean

eponym: Oceanus, Greek Titan

The Greek gods, like Cupid and Apollo, may be familiar to many. But the Titans are not as well known. The Greeks believed that the Titans were giants who originally ruled the earth before being overthrown by the gods. The publisher of this book, Hyperion, borrowed its name from one of the Titans, Hyperion, who was the father of Aurora (goddess of the dawn), Selene (the moon goddess), and Helios (the sun god).

One of these strong, powerful Titans was Oceanus. Oceanus was lord of a river named Ocean, which was believed to have encircled the entire earth. Now the word *ocean* refers generally to the large bodies of salt water that cover approximately three-fourths of the earth's surface.

wellington

eponym: Duke of Wellington

Arthur Wellesley, first duke of Wellington, is best remembered as the English general who led the victorious allied forces against Napoléon Bonaparte at the Battle of Waterloo in 1815.

The duke also had the honor of having several pieces of clothing and furniture named after him. There are Wellington coats, hats, trousers, and boots, and there's even a Wellington chest of drawers. Best known of these are, no doubt, the high leather boots called Wellingtons, which cover the knee in the front and are cut away in the back. Nowadays there are also tall, waterproof rubber boots called Wellies for short.

jersey

toponym: Isle of Jersey, Channel Islands, England

While the men of Jodhpur kept cool in baggy pants, residents of the Isle of Jersey, in the English Channel, had the opposite dilemma. They needed clothing that would keep them warm and dry on an island known for its blustery, wet weather. To meet their needs, residents began knitting shirts and sweaters that became known as jerseys. A knitted sweater in England is called a jersey pullover, not a sweater.

The first jerseys knitted on the island were made of wool. Wool was used because it tends to help hold in the body's heat even when the material gets wet. Today *jersey* is a general term for any knitted fabric, whether it's wool, cotton, silk, or synthetic. Jersey tops and separates are soft and comfortable, which is why they're often worn by people who are relaxing or playing sports.

sleaze

toponym: Silesia

What's an adjective like *sleazy,* which means cheap and vulgar, doing in the clothing section? And where is Silesia? It's an interesting word-history tale even though it's peppered with a few holes.

Silesia is a region in east central Europe, formerly in Germany, now part of the Czech Republic and Poland. As far back as 1670 there are written accounts telling of a fine Silesian linen cloth woven in this area. The cloth was also called Sleasie.

Since Sleasie cloth was thin, it wore out quickly and offered little protection in cold weather. This led to critical references to thin, worthless Sleasie cloth. Over time the name of a cloth that was originally associated with quality shifted to mean something inferior. In the late 1960s a British publication wrote that London's Soho area was a place noted for its "brazen sleaze."

cardigan

eponym: Earl of Cardigan

Perhaps some readers are familiar with these often quoted lines from the poem "The Charge of the Light Brigade" by Alfred, Lord Tennyson: "Into the valley of Death / Rode the six hundred."

These lines describe the ill-fated charge of 600 English cavalrymen, in October 1854, at the Battle of Balaklava during the Crimean War. Over half of the ill-equipped English forces were killed while charging the powerful Russian guns.

The English officer who led the charge was James Thomas Brudenell, the seventh earl of Cardigan. But the earl is probably more famous for his habit of wearing the sweater jacket of knitted wool that now carries his name, the cardigan, than for his military deeds.

raglan

eponym: Baron Raglan

It seems highly unlikely, but the names of two English soldiers who fought in the same battle gave rise to two recognizable fashion terms, *cardigan* and *raglan.*

Did you ever have a cardigan sweater with sleeves that were sewn on a diagonal from the underarm to the neck? These sleeves are called raglan sleeves. And the man behind the name was none other than the earl of Cardigan's commanding officer at the battle of Balaklava, Fitzroy James Henry Somerset, also known as Baron Raglan.

And like the earl of Cardigan, Baron Raglan is better remembered for the cut of his overcoat sleeves than for any battles he fought.

fuchsias on friday

magnet

toponym: Magnesia

People with magnetic personalities attract a lot of friends to them, the same way magnets attract bits of iron or steel.

Long ago, the Greeks noticed that certain stones naturally attracted metal. Since these stones were first mined in an area called Magnesia, the Greeks referred to them as "stones of Magnesia." Our word *magnet* comes from the place name Magnesia, which is now part of Turkey. Later, scientists referred to these natural magnets as magnetite or lodestone.

In 1819 magnets began to receive their magnetic properties electrically, when a current was passed through pieces of iron or steel. A compass's needle is magnetic and responds to the earth's magnetism by always pointing north.

zephyr

eponym: Zephyrus, Greek god

Another name for a gentle breeze, especially one from the west, is zephyr. In ancient Greece, Zephyrus was the god of the west wind.

In Greek legend winds do more than ruffle leaves and fill sails. They play an active role in the lives of heroes, heroines, and villains. According to one story, a king and queen reluctantly followed an oracle's instructions and abandoned their beautiful, unmarried daughter, Psyche, on a rocky hill. Psyche, they were told, would be carried off by a serpent as his wife. But Zephyrus took pity on Psyche and lifted her up with his sweet, mild west wind. The wind delivered her to a beautiful place, where she met Cupid, the god of love, who himself fell in love with the mortal Psyche.

atlas

One of the Titans who led the losing fight against the gods was named Atlas. Atlas was mighty and strong, which is why one bodybuilder adopted the name Charles Atlas when he launched his bodybuilding school.

When the gods overthrew the Titans, Zeus punished Atlas by forcing him to support the heavens on his shoulders. You've probably seen illustrations of the well-built Atlas bowed under the weight of the world resting on his muscular shoulders.

In the sixteenth century, a geographer living in what is now Belgium included a drawing of Atlas on the front page of his collection of maps. From this association, *atlas* became the term now used to refer to a book of maps.

iris

eponym: Iris, Greek goddess

Are your eyes brown? If they are, that means the small, opaque part of your eye, the iris, is brown. Although nobody has naturally colored rainbow eyes, the Greek word *iris* means "rainbow."

The Greek goddess Iris was known as the rainbow goddess. She was also a messenger for the gods, especially when they were up to mischief. Iris wore a multicolored cloak that trailed across the sky in a rainbow curve. The rainbow provided Iris with a handy bridge over which she could travel.

The flower with the tall thin leaves and showy flower that comes in a rainbow of colors also gets its name from the goddess Iris.

fuchsia

eponym: Leonhard Fuchs

Over the past four centuries, hundreds of plants have received their names from people, including the scientists who first discovered or took a great interest in them. Lately, politicians, movie stars, and musicians have inspired plant names. There's even a variety of ornamental grass called Heavy Metal.

Many people display fuchsia in hanging baskets during the summer. Hummingbirds, in particular, are drawn to their red drooping flowers. In tropical America fuchsias grow wild as either shrubs, trees, or climbers. Fuchsias were named after the German botanist and physician Leonhard Fuchs, who devoted himself to their cultivation during the sixteenth century.

poinsettia

eponym: Doctor Joel Poinsett

The red plant that fills florists' windows at Christmastime is the poinsettia, considered the traditional holiday plant in the United States for over a century.

The poinsettia grows outdoors as a bush in warm climates. Three centuries ago in Mexico, Franciscan monks began to incorporate poinsettias in their Christmas celebrations. Mexicans called the plant *flor de la Noche Buena,* "flower of the blessed night," because its star-shaped blooms reminded them of the Star of Bethlehem.

After President Martin Van Buren named Doctor Poinsett first minister to Mexico, Poinsett brought a few of the showy plants back to the United States. Immediately adopted as the plant of Christmas, the poinsettia was named to honor the American diplomat.

queen anne's lace   eponym: Queen Anne of England

Although many flowers were named after the scientists who first cultivated them, other flowers got their names from famous people, such as members of royal families. A well-known flower with a royal name is Queen Anne's lace. Often seen along fencerows and roadsides, the white, lacy wildflower is a botanical cousin to the ordinary garden carrot (notice their similar feathery foliage).

The most widely accepted story behind the plant's name goes back 300 years, to the reign of England's queen Anne. The queen challenged her royal ladies-in-waiting to embroider a fabric equal in beauty to the lacy pattern of a tall white flower that grew in the palace garden. Talented as they were, the needleworkers failed. The beauty of the wildflower won out, and the queen's name was thereafter associated with the delicate flower.

Another theory suggests that the flower got its name from Saint Anne, the grandmother of Jesus and patron saint of lacemakers.

sisal   toponym: Sisal, Yucatán, Mexico

If you've ever tied a package with a strong scratchy brown cord, you probably used sisal. *Sisal* is another word with its roots in Mexico. The fibers used to make sisal come from two tropical plants whose swordlike leaves are dried and twisted.

Sisal fibers, from 20 to 50 inches long, are strong and used chiefly to make twine and cording. In addition sisal is used to make mats, hammocks, and many other decorative objects in Mexico and the West Indies, where the plant grows.

volt

eponym: Alessandro Volta

Does it seem as if you're always running out of batteries? Many of the everyday items we depend on use batteries, from watches and cameras to portable radios and flashlights.

The man who invented the first electrical battery, called a voltaic pile, was an Italian scientist named Alessandro Volta. Napoléon Bonaparte made Volta a count after the emperor proclaimed himself king of Italy. The unit for measuring electromotive force is called a volt after Count Volta.

fahrenheit

eponym: Gabriel D. Fahrenheit

Did someone ever stick a cold thermometer under your tongue when you didn't feel well? If the red line on the thermometer rose a few degrees beyond 98.6, the normal body temperature, you probably had a fever.

Thermometers have been around for centuries. The very first one, an alcohol thermometer, was made in 1593 by the Italian astronomer and physicist Galileo, but it measured only large temperature changes.

The invention was greatly improved when, in 1714, a German physicist named Gabriel Fahrenheit built an accurate sealed thermometer using mercury. On the scale that took the scientist's name water freezes at 32 degrees and boils at 212 degrees.

mercury

eponym: Mercury, Roman god

Gabriel Fahrenheit filled his thermometers with a silvery white metallic element known as mercury. The physicist chose mercury for two reasons: it's the only metal that stays liquid at moderate temperatures, and it expands and contracts in regular degrees depending on the temperature.

Because mercury flows so freely it was named after the Roman god Mercury, the fleet-footed messenger. (The element is also called quicksilver.) A famous statue depicts the god Mercury wearing sandals and a hat with wings. The god needed these wings to respond quickly to Zeus's commands to carry messages. In the statue Mercury also carries a caduceus, a staff entwined with two snakes, which was later adopted by physicians as their symbol.

wednesday, thursday, friday   eponyms: Woden, Thor, and Freya, Scandinavian gods

We also have mythology to thank for the names of three of our weekdays. All three days were named after two gods and a goddess from the same Scandinavian family.

In Norse mythology, the chief god, comparable to the Greek god Zeus, was named Wōden, or Odin in Anglo-Saxon. From his name came "Wōden's day," or Wednesday.

Thursday, or "Thor's day," was named after Odin's son, Thor. Strong, red-haired Thor is most known for his iron gloves and magic hammer.

The sixth day of the week, Friday, or "Freya's day," got its name from the supreme Scandinavian goddess, Freya, Odin's wife and Thor's mother. Freya was the Norse goddess of love and death.

cheap china in a parchment palace

gadget

Americans, in particular, a gadget for just about any several dictionaries under obscure." One suggestion is that word *gachette,* which means "lock-

eponym: Emile Gaget

seem to love gadgets. In fact, there's job you can name. But a check of *gadget* reads, "origin unknown or *gadget* evolved from the French ing mechanism."

Another, more colorful explanation, also of French origin, concerns a man named Emile Gaget (gah-jay), whose firm, Gaget, Gauthier and Company, built the 152-foot-high copper Statue of Liberty in their Paris workshop.

To honor the statue's October 28, 1886, inauguration ceremony in New York Harbor, the industrious Emile Gaget sold souvenir replicas of the statue in Paris. These miniatures were nicknamed "gagets" after their creator. However, Americans living in Paris pronounced the word with an added *d,* which is how *gadget* entered our language.

artesian

toponym: Artois, France

If you ever drew water from a well, you probably pumped the water from underground. Artesian wells are different. The water in an artesian well stays above the surface of the ground. Artesian wells only occur under certain geological conditions.

When a well hole is drilled into the ground and water gets trapped by surrounding clay or dense rock, the water cannot pass through the dense material. Under pressure the water then rises through the drilled opening. Sometimes an artesian well sends up an initial fountain of water hundreds of feet into the air.

The word *artesian* comes from a province in northern France called Artois, where the first artesian well occurred naturally over 900 years ago.

bungalow

toponym: Bengal, India

As we already read, the British occupied India for 200 years, ending in 1947. As a direct result of this occupation, some 26,000 Indian words were absorbed into the English language. Among these are a few eponyms and toponyms. We've already discussed the toponyms *jodhpur* and *dungaree*. Another is *bungalow*.

Indian bungalows are one-story houses, usually with a thatched roof, and a balcony or veranda. They were especially common in the northeastern Indian province of Bengal. The Hindi word for Bengal is *bangla,* which became *bungalow* when used by the British to describe the house style. Early in this century builders constructed thousands of one-and-a-half-story bungalows in the United States.

lobby

toponym: House of Commons, London, England

If you live in an apartment building, there is probably a lobby downstairs at the entrance. This area was named after an outer room in the British Parliament's House of Commons called the lobby.

Lobby took on another meaning in the United States during the 1830s. At that time people tried to influence the decisions of congressional legislators. For the most part these people peddled their opinions in the lobbies of government offices. This led to their being dubbed lobbyists. Today's full-time, salaried lobbyists are very much a part of our political process.

attic

If you live in a house, there may be an attic between the top story ceiling and the roof. Some attics are just big enough to crawl through; others are large enough to be turned into spare rooms.

The word *attic* means "Athenian," or relating to the Greek city Athens. In ancient Greece, Athens was part of a region called Attica. Attic was also a simple, elegant style of architecture. Attic-style buildings featured a smaller second story or a room on top of a taller story, just under the roof.

china

toponym: China

Hands down, china is the most frequently used toponym in the English language. There's a cupboard with shelves called a china closet and a white artists' pigment known as China white. But most of us use the term in conjunction with expensive porcelain vases and dishes. In fact, many people display their prized china in a china closet.

Nearly 3,000 years ago, the Chinese were making a kind of earthenware through which light could pass. The Portuguese, who first brought this earthenware to Europe, named it porcelain. Later porcelain became known as china after the Persian word *chini,* which evolved in England, first as *chiney.* In the middle of the eighteenth century, the English began to produce bone china, called bone because it contained bone ash.

Can you think of any other terms that contain *china?*

cheap

toponym: Cheapside, London, England

The word *cheap* originally did not mean a bargain, nor did it originate from a person or a place. As it developed, however, *cheap* became a toponym after all. So it's included here.

The Old English root of *cheap* was *cēap* (pronounced with a soft *c*), which meant "to barter, buy, or sell." By the late sixteenth century, *cēaping* spots in London were centered around Cheapside and Eastcheap. Since shoppers going to Cheapside and Eastcheap bargained to get merchandise at greatly reduced prices, *cheap's* original meaning of trading or buying was narrowed to mean specifically something bought at a low price.

capitol

Is Washington, D.C., our nation's capit*al* or capit*ol*? Congress meets in the Capitol Building on Capitol Hill, in Washington, D.C., the capital city of the United States.

In the English language, *capitol* refers only to the building or buildings where the legislature meets. *Capitol* got its name from the Capitoline Hill, which was

the highest point in ancient Rome and site of the Temple of Jupiter (the Roman name for the Greek god Zeus).

Capital has several meanings: serious, excellent, net worth, and the city that serves as the seat of a state's or country's government. Unlike *capitol, capital* was not named for the famous Roman hill.

palace

toponym: Palatine Hill, Rome, Italy

Let's climb another famous hill in Rome to examine the origins of the word *palace*. Around 50 B.C. the first emperor of Rome, Caesar Augustus, built a huge complex at the top of the Palatine Hill overlooking Rome. The buildings combined living space with a governmental center, the equivalent of our White House and the Capitol Building together.

Our English word *palace* came directly from the French word *palais,* which had its roots in Augustus's monumental structure with the great view.

coach

toponym: Kocs, Hungary

Coach is one of the few English words that came from Hungary. It was in the village of Kocs that the first horse-drawn coach was invented in the fifteenth century. In Hungarian the coaches were known as *kocsi szekér* (kō-chē´ sĕ-kar). That tongue twister was shortened to *kocs,* then, finally, became in English *coach.*

Coach has taken a long ride in the English language. In addition to its original meaning, *coach* also refers to people who train singers, dancers, and athletes, and even to economy class on an airplane. But all coaches, whether stagecoaches or coaches who train people for the stage, have their origin in the same Hungarian town.

ghetto

toponym: Il Geto, Venice, Italy

Today *ghetto* generally refers to an urban area where lower-income ethnic minorities live. The first ghetto was set on the Venetian island of Giudecca, nearly five centuries ago.

The source for the toponym *ghetto* was Il Geto, the nickname for Giudecca. After a decree in 1516 by the Venetian city fathers, all people of Jewish origin were confined to separate communities on Il Geto. The practice of segregating Jewish people grew throughout Europe, and these segregated areas were called ghettos, after Il Geto.

lumber

eponym: Lombard

We read earlier that galoshes got their name from the Gauls. From another ancient tribe, the Lombards, comes our word *lumber*. The Lombards were originally known as Longobardus, which means "long beard." But by the sixteenth century, an anglicized version of the name, *lumber*, referred to pieces of wood and other odds and ends.

There's no clear explanation as to why wood became associated with this group of people. One possible reason is that the Lombards often had pawn shops, where they collected and sold an odd assortment of wooden articles. This junkyard of sorts may have been the very first lumberyard.

parchment
toponym: Pergamum, Greece

Scholars in ancient Greece and Egypt were able to study at two of the most splendid libraries ever known. The two libraries in Pergamum, Greece, and Alexandria, Egypt, contained books written on sheets of papyrus made from a plant that grows along Egypt's Nile River.

One day the Egyptian pharaoh, jealous of the Greek library's growing reputation, refused to deliver any Egyptian papyrus to Pergamum to make books. So the industrious people of Pergamum came up with an alternative to papyrus by stretching, scraping, and softening the skins of goats and sheep. The resulting sheets were called *pergamēnē,* meaning "from Pergamum." In French *pergamēnē* became *parchemin* and, later, in English, *parchment.*

venetian blind
toponym: Venice, Italy

Venetian blinds were invented in Persia. So why weren't they called Persian blinds?

The Italian people living on the collection of islands called Venice didn't invent the blinds, but they made them so popular that the toponymous sun shades have been called venetian blinds for nearly five centuries. In their homes and shops Venetians hung horizontal slats, which could be raised and lowered, in open and closed positions. The blinds gave them privacy and protected them from the oppressive afternoon heat and sun.

diesel
eponym: Rudolf Diesel

Did you ever wonder why long-distance freight trucks fill up at different gas-station pumps than cars? Large trucks have diesel engines that are different from the gasoline engines in cars. In 1892, German engineer Rudolf Diesel filed a patent for the engine that carries his name.

Gasoline engines run by spark ignition: a mixture of fuel and air expands under pressure and ignites the fuel by electric spark. Diesel engines work by compression ignition: the heat of compressed air in the cylinder ignites the fuel.

Fuel for diesel engines is less refined than the fuel used in gasoline engines. But tractor trailer trucks use diesel fuel, because it gives them more power per gallon to haul their heavy weight.

macadam

eponym: John L. McAdam

Nearly two hundred years ago a Scottish engineer named John L. McAdam paved the way for a revolution of his own. He did it by devising a new way of building roads. McAdam placed three layers of small stones onto well-drained soil. The weight of the passing traffic crushed the stones into the surface, making dirt roads smoother and more durable.

These roads were called macadams after the engineer's name. In the pre-freeway age, macadam roads held up well under horse-and-buggy travel. But the heavy traffic of faster moving automobiles dug up the small stones and sent clouds of dust into passengers' faces. Soon, roadways paved with asphalt took the place of most macadam roads.

gauze

toponym: Gaza, Palestine

If you've ever trained for a marathon jogging down a macadam road, you might need ointment and gauze to soothe blisters and aching joints. Gauze, a thick, transparent cloth woven from linen, cotton, or even silk, is used to make clothing and mosquito netting. Another name for surgical gauze is cheesecloth.

Gauze takes its name from the place where it was first made, Gaza, part of the contested lands of Palestine.

mall

toponym: The Mall, London, England

Cruising the mall has turned into a popular pastime among Americans of all ages. The latest and biggest malls include hundreds of stores, fountains, and even children's amusements. In the United States the first mall was built in 1956, near Minneapolis. However, the first large-scale enclosed shopping structure may have been Italy's famous Galleria in Milan, built more than a hundred years ago and still open for business.

Before *mall* became synonymous with an enclosed commercial space, the term referred to a long tree-lined promenade. Both malls take their name from a former London field (now a street) called Pall-Mall and later just the Mall. The field was called Pall-Mall because the grassy lawn was a playing field for a game invented in the seventeenth century called pall-mall. Pall-mall players use a wooden mallet to hit a ball through a metal arch.

bibliography

Ammer, Christine. *Fighting Words*. New York: Laurel/Dell, 1990.

Beeching, Cyril Leslie. *A Dictionary of Eponyms*. New York: Oxford University Press, 1983.

Brandreth, Gyles. *The Joy of Lex*. New York: Quill, 1983.

Funk, Wilfred. *Word Origins and Their Romantic Stories*. New York: Wilfred Funk, 1950.

Holt, Alfred H. *Phrase and Word Origins: A Study of Familiar Expressions*. 2d ed. New York: Dover, 1961.

Jacobson, John. *Toposaurus, A Humorous Treasury of Toponyms*. New York: Wiley, 1990.

Oxford Dictionary of English Etymology. Oxford: Clarendon Press, 1966.

Panati, Charles. *Panati's Browser's Book of Beginnings*. Boston: Houghton Mifflin, 1984.

————*Panati's Extraordinary Origins of Everyday Things*. New York: Harper & Row, 1987.

Random House Dictionary. New York: Random House, 1983.

Shipley, Joseph T. *Dictionary of Word Origins*. New York: Philosophical Library, 1945.

Tuleja, Tad. *Marvelous Monikers*. New York: Harmony, 1990.

Viney, Nigel. *Dictionary of Toponyms*. London: The Library Association, 1986 (out of print).

Webster's New Collegiate Dictionary. Springfield, Massachusetts: G.C. Merriam Company, 1977 (out of print).